The SCARiEST MONSTER in the Whole Wide World

Pamela Mayer · illustrated by Lydia Monks

G. P. Putnam's Sons · New York

For Richard . . . of course!

P. M.

For the scariest monster in the
whole wide world—
Mr. Frazer Hudson.

L. M.

Text copyright © 2001 by Pamela Mayer
Illustrations copyright © 2001 by Lydia Monks
All rights reserved. This book, or parts thereof, may not be reproduced
in any form without permission in writing from the publisher,
G. P. PUTNAM'S SONS,
a division of Penguin Putnam Books for Young Readers,
345 Hudson Street, New York, NY 10014.
G. P. Putnam's Sons, Reg. U.S. Pat. & Tm. Off. Published simultaneously in Canada.
Printed in Hong Kong by South China Printing Co. (1988) Ltd.
Text set in 14 point Adriatic
The art was done in acrylic paint, paper montage, and colored pencils.
Library of Congress Cataloging-in-Publication Data
Mayer, Pamela. The scariest monster in the whole wide world / Pamela Mayer;
illustrated by Lydia Monks. p. cm. Summary: Thea's parents do not want her
to dress up as a scary monster for the Halloween costume parade, but with
Grandma's help she surprises them. [1. Costume—Fiction. 2. Halloween—Fiction.
3. Monsters—Fiction. 4. Grandmothers—Fiction.] I. Monks, Lydia, ill. II. Title.
PZ7.M463 Sc 2001 [E]—dc21 00-041549
ISBN 0-399-23459-4
1 2 3 4 5 6 7 8 9 10
First Impression

Last Halloween
Thea Dewhickey won second
prize at the costume parade.
    Her mother and father were so proud.
    This Halloween they wanted her to come in first.

Mrs. Dewhickey placed the photograph of Thea in her prize-winning fairy princess costume on the kitchen table. "Look at her little feet in the silver slippers!" she said.

"And her ringlets under her golden crown—ah, me!" Mr. Dewhickey sighed.

"What do you want to be this year, precious?" they asked.

"I want to be—"

"A butterfly," Mrs. Dewhickey interrupted.
"Pale blue leotard, filmy chiffon wings..."

"No, Thea should
be a Spanish dancer,
all red and black ruffles.
That will really wow the judges,"
Mr. Dewhickey said.

"Which do you prefer, darling?"
they asked.

"I want to be the scariest monster in the whole wide world!" Thea said.

Mr. and Mrs. Dewhickey were too surprised to speak.

"I want claws and fangs and green scales and blood dripping off the corners of my mouth, and maybe even an ax coming out of my head. Can I, Mommy and Daddy? Huh? Please? May I?"

Just then the oven timer went off. Mrs. Dewhickey jumped
from her chair with a cry of "Eek!"

"Oh, boy—pumpkin pie!" Thea said.

Mr. Dewhickey took the pie from the oven.

But Thea was the only one who felt like eating.

The next afternoon Mr. and Mrs. Dewhickey took Thea
downtown to the Halloween Superstore. They hurried toward
the racks of beautiful costumes, but Thea tugged on their hands.
"What I like is over here," she said.

Your
One Stop Shop
for
Halloween
Party Favors
Home Decor
Makeup
and much more!

"How do I look?" she asked.

"Aaargh!" Mrs. Dewhickey screamed.

A salesman came over. "Would you like to see some great accessories to go with that mask?" he asked.

"Not today," Mr. Dewhickey said, and he led them out of the store.

On the way home Mrs. Dewhickey wiped a tear from her eye. "Mary Lou Von Halper is going as Bo-Peep. Her mother has been working on that costume for six months."

"Now, now," Mr. Dewhickey said.

"The scariest monster in the whole wide world could never win first prize at the costume parade," Mrs. Dewhickey said sadly. "What are we going to do?"

For the next several days Mr. and Mrs. Dewhickey visited
costume shops, brought home sewing patterns, and leafed through
mail-order catalogs. But whenever they showed Thea a costume,
all she said was, "I want to be the scariest monster in the whole wide
world! Can we get my costume tomorrow? Huh? Please?"

It was time to call for expert advice.
Grandma arrived the next morning.

"Boo!" she said.
"Grandma!"
"Sugar Plum!"

Grandma and Thea hugged.

"Now, you'll help us take care of Thea's costume—"
Mr. Dewhickey said.

"Don't worry," Grandma said. "Look, it's been ages
since I've spent a day alone with Thea. Why don't you two
go out?"

Thea and Grandma spent all morning getting ready for Halloween. They decorated the house and were just dipping the last apple into caramel sauce when Grandma said, "Tell me about your Halloween costume."

"I want to be the scariest monster in the whole wide world!" Thea told Grandma about the claws, the fangs, the green scales, and the ax.

"Sounds good to me," said Grandma.

"You know," Thea said, "sometimes I get the feeling Mommy and Daddy don't want me to be a scary monster at all."

"I have an idea," Grandma said. "Are there any costume shops around here?"

She and Thea raced downtown to the Halloween Superstore.
They soon found everything they needed.

Fortunately, Grandma was a whiz
at sewing. She whipped up Thea's costume
in no time, and finished her other projects
just as Mr. and Mrs. Dewhickey came
home that evening.

"Surprise!" Thea said.

Mr. and Mrs. Dewhickey certainly WERE surprised. This was not what they had in mind, but then Grandma told them what else she had made.

On Halloween Thea had the most fun she had ever had
marching in the costume parade.

First prize went to Mary Lou Von Halper
for her Bo-Peep costume.
Thea did not win a prize.
But Mr. and Mrs. Dewhickey did.

The judges thought the butterfly costume Grandma made for Mrs. Dewhickey was dreamy. And Mr. Dewhickey's Spanish dancer costume with its red ruffled shirt and black pants really wowed them.

Thea was so proud.

Maybe next year her mother and father would come in first.